CARRIED

Carri Ed

AuthorHouse™
1663 Liberty Drive
Bloomington, IN 47403
www.authorhouse.com
Phone: 1-800-839-8640

Published by AuthorHouse 7/26/2013

ISBN: 978-1-4817-7806-0 (sc)
ISBN: 978-1-4817-7805-3 (e)

This book is printed on acid-free paper.

Author's Note

This book is based on my own perceptions of my past, present and future. My experiences are based on my memories, research, and documented court records.

I have not disclosed names, locations or identifying characteristics to protect the innocent, especially my family. They have been through enough.

I have not corrected punctuation or grammar in this book. It is important to me that readers know you do not have to be "perfect" to write a book and get your message out there. Be real and come as you are!

I dedicate this book to the people I have hurt, the victims of my choices, my parents who never gave up and my beautiful caring daughters. May God grant you all peace.

I was born in an unwed mothers home. My birth mother was sixteen years old when I was born. She was from a very poor family. I was told she had six siblings and is German and Irish.

She made a very wise decision in placing me for adoption. I am very grateful she did. I was placed in a loving, Christian home with three older siblings. They were ages seven, six and five years old when I arrived.

My birth father was twenty years old when I was born. I was told he was also from a poor family and had eleven siblings. He is Native American and English.

At the time of my birth, he was on probation for burglary. In the year I was born, he had no rights in the decision to keep or place me for adoption. It was totally my birth mother's decision.

At a very young age, I noticed I looked different from my siblings. They were also very close in age and I was five years younger. They looked Native and I looked totally white with freckles.

My adoptive father is also Native American but from another tribe. My adoptive mother is also German and Irish like my birth mother.

As soon as I realized something was different I asked questions. My adoptive mother told me, I was adopted.

Knowing I was adopted made me feel special. I liked being adopted. Besides I was the only one in the family that was adopted and I really liked that.

During sibling rivalry I would yell to my sisters and my brother and say, “so, if mom and dad would not have gotten married none of you would be here but I still would be”! That comment really made me feel like I had one up on them.

I used to brag to other kids and say, “I am adopted”. I was proud. Until... the girls in my neighborhood told me my adoptive family was not my real family. They told me my real mother did not want me that is why she gave me away. That my real mother did not love me. That comment hurt and was the beginning of my feelings of inadequacies and low self-esteem. I began to believe I was not good enough.

My adoptive mother to me was my real mother. How dare they say she wasn’t. My adoptive mother told me over and over how much she loved me. She told me I did belong in this exact family and it was God who had put me with them. God doesn’t make mistakes and I belong with them. She also told me she did not have to adopt me that she could have waited for a different baby but she wanted me. So did my brother, sisters and my dad. I wanted to believe her but I couldn't. I thought she was just saying that because that is what moms are suppose to say. I began to feel out of place. A hole felt like it was forming in my heart. The more I thought about what the girls said to me, the bigger the hole became.

Psalm 139:16 says: "You saw me before I was born. Everyday of my life was recorded in your book. Every moment was laid out before a single day had passed."

If only I had known this verse then. But how could I have known when I was probably five years old.

The girls in my neighborhood were all from the same family. The ones who told me this and there were four of them. They told me alot of lies. So when the girl closest to my age told me things her dad was doing to her, I did not believe her. Besides I could not imagine a dad doing things like that to their own daughter. Dads do not do such things. That was something I could not even comprehend. That was gross. My dad was the best. I admired and thought the world of him. He was amazing to me. So thoughtful, so patient, so understanding, so handsome. I was proud of my dad. I would watch him for hours while he cleaned the garage. I said watch him, I did not say help him. I am a kid at this time you know. And, of course, he never said a word when I took the wheels off of his lawn mower to put on my go-cart. He was a man of few words but when he did say something he said it with love, concern and a strong meaning. So no, I could not believe that girl when she said that about her dad.

Those girls did odd things. One day they put me and one of their sisters in the shed and make us take off our clothes. I could hear my mom yelling for me to come home and the girls would not give me back my clothes. Finally they did and I went home. My mom never knew and I never told her.

A few years later it came out that the girls were telling the truth. Their dad was molesting them. No wonder they acted so odd and did strange things. They had lied so much to me that when they did tell the truth it was hard to believe. Like the little boy who cried wolf, I guess.

Years and years later I realized I had been "touched" by him too. I slept over at their house one night and woke up with a hickey. I blamed it on one of the girls because she was the only one around me when I had been sleeping.

Later in life, I started to have flashbacks of their dad's bright blue eyes. I knew he was the one who gave me that hickey. That would explain why night after night he would come to my parents house. He wanted to find out if I was going to tell on him. Little did he know I had repressed it.

Then, I started to have flashbacks about going to their basement. He had two of his daughters in the basement also and the one closest to my age looked so sad. I went in the little room and I remember him telling me to promise not to tell my mom. Why? Tell her what? I had blocked it out so I did not know what he meant. I know now. He meant not to tell that he had been molesting them in the basement that day. I believe he molested me too. Now I know why my friend looked so sad.

The girls parents got divorced. This was my first experience with divorce. I was amazed that many years later those girls had forgiven their dad. I could not understand that either. How awful to hate your dad for what he did to you but yet love him because he is your dad. Amazing girls in that aspect.

I went to a Lutheran Grade School and High School. I was given the best education offered. I was a cheerleader, ran track and liked to go to school. I was a talker and most times had my desk at the back of the classroom. Attention. I wanted all the attention even if it was negative.

In kindergarten, I committed my first "crime". I stoled another child's picture. I crossed off his name and put my name on it. I liked it better than mine and wanted to bring it to my mom. Even at age five I thought the things I did were not good enough. When my mom saw the picture she knew instantly what I had done. She then explained to me she did not want another child's picture she only wanted mine. I was so happy because that meant she liked me.

So the next day I brought my picture home and she hung it up. I was so proud. I was even more happy because I had made my mother happy.

Around age eight I knew how important it was to be baptized and how important God is. I also knew my little cousins were not baptized. That concerned me. As young as I was, I was very smart. So, I did a little research in books and found were it talked about baptism and read I did not have to be a pastor or preacher to perform a baptism. I was so happy because that meant I could baptize my little cousins. So, I did. I baptized them in the bathroom sink. It was the happiest day for me because that meant if anything happened to us we were all going to heaven. I never did get to baptize my youngest cousin. I still wonder if that is the reason she turned Gothic. If only I could have baptized her too, maybe she could have worn brighter colors.

My grade school years were normal. Every summer the girls in my class would go to a christian summer camp for a week. It was so much fun. All of us also belong to a bowling league.

I had a best friend in sixth, seventh and eighth grades. One summer at camp we got matching t-shirts with our names on the back of them. I thought the world of my best friend. She really was the best.

At fourteen years old I met a boy. He is eighteen years old. He likes me. The other kids in the neighborhood tell me that he wants to talk to me. I go outside and talk to him. He is in highschool. Cool. I am his girlfriend now. Why shouldn't I be his girlfriend we talked for a whole hour.

Two months later and we are still together. My parents do not like him. Figures. They do not know anything. They hate me anyway because I am not their real kid. They tell me not to see him anymore. Whatever. We sneak to see each other. My parents are trying to ruin my life. They act like they know everything. Forget them.

I am so tired. All I wanna do is sleep. I go to school and come home and go directly to sleep. I do this everyday over and over. I do not do my homework. I can't, I am too tired. I sleep in my moms bed because it is so comfortable. I barely eat. I am too tired to eat but then how did I gain ten pounds in two and a half months? I do not wanna be fat.

I worry I am going to be fat. I can not be fat because no one in my class will like me if I am fat. Now my teacher is lecturing me about my failing grades. Who cares! They were low anyway. I have a boyfriend I do not have time for studying. Oh great, now I will be fat and dumb! Not to forget lazy because all I wanna do is sleep.

My boyfriend calls. We still are not allowed to see each other. I will sneak and see him tomorrow after school. After I go and see him I will sneak home before my mom gets home from work. She is hardly ever home because she works alot. She is a work aholic so it is easy to beat her home. Oh, it is Tuesday and my dad works late on Tuesdays. Good.

I made it home. No one knows I was gone. I am hungry. I am afraid to eat. I do not want to get fatter. I eat chicken noodle soup. The next day I buy Dexatrim diet pills. I take them for two weeks. They do not work. I gained two more pounds. I tell my friend from school that I think I am pregnant. It is okay if I am, it is no big deal. I like babies. Babies are cute as long as it doesn't look like the father. He is ugly.

My friend and I go to the Free Clinic. We sneak away from the basketball game at school to go get my test done. I take the test. It is positive. The nurse says I am high risk because I am only fourteen. I ask her if that means I will die. She says no, I will not die and gives me my due date. My friend and I leave to go back to the basketball game. We make it back to the school just before my dad shows up to pick me up. Lucky. I am due in August just four days after my fifteenth birthday. Cool. We can celebrate our birthdays together. this will be fun.

My friend and I tell my teacher. She says I should tell my mother right away. I go home from school and when my momgets home from work I tell her I am pregnant. She starts to cry. Why is she crying? What is the big deal? Babies are cute. She likes babies so why would she cry? My dad just came home.

My mom tells my dad. My dad starts to cry. Now I start to cry. I have never in my life seen my dad cry. What kind of a person makes their own dad cry? A terrible awful person that is who.

My Lutheran High School calls my mom. I can not come back to school. My pregnancy makes the school look bad. What about my friends? My mom fights to make the school let me stay. They refuse. They can not have this type of behavior at their school. I now have to go to school for teen mothers. It is not so bad. Everyone at the pregnant school is pregnant. I have to get there on the city bus. Everyone on the bus stares A baby having a baby. I am dirty. I am bad. I broke up with the father. He wants to take and keep my baby. Is he crazy? No way! Not my baby! No one is taking my baby from me! My sisters are in college and they came home for the weekend. My mom tells them. My oldest sister is furious. She says she is the oldest and is suppose to have the first baby. She ignores me. My mom makes her be nice to me. My other sister is nice but feels sorry for me. My brother will not talk to me at all. I was his baby sister and look what I have done to our family. My friends do not call me. My mom hides me in big jackets. We go to other churches and not our own so her friends do not see me. I am an embarrassment to everyone. I still do not see the big deal. It is only a baby. I can not comprehend the effect this has on others not even on myself.

My mom calls a social worker from an adoption agency. The same agency I was adopted through. An adoption agent came to see me. She gave me information on my own adoption and asked me if I would consider placing my baby for adoption. No way! I am not giving up my baby for adoption. This crazy old woman was talking non-sense. After a few more times of talking to her I started to like this lady. I could tell her things I could not and would not tell my mother. My mother was mean and hated me. She was out to get me. I was developing a resentment towards my adoptive mother. I told her many times when I was mad at her that I wish she never would have adopted me. All she ever said to that comment was, "I am sorry you feel that way because I am happy I adopted you because I love you very much." Blah! She would say that. She reassured me over and over how much she loved me. She lies, I do not believe a word she says.

My mother was a very loving mother. She spent time reading to me, tucking me in at night. She said she spent more time with me than she did the other kids. She was a very hardworking woman and spent long hours working to give us kids the things we needed and wanted. While she thought about her childrens future such as college education etc. I could not see that. I thought see was gone because she did not like me. Even as a child my thinking was extremely distorted. While she wanted to protect me from dating loser and keeping a baby I was too young to raise, I saw it as her trying to ruin my life. Actually, she was trying to save it.

Then my mean mother started telling people I was giving up my baby for adoption. I did not say that! She did! So she let me get a dog. I was allowed to buy it myself with my babysitting job money. I was so proud. I bought a Golden Retriever. I had got my drive for work from my mother. At age nine I had made business cards and past them out all over the area we lived in. I liked to work and earn money on my own. I would lie and say I was eleven because I knew I had a better chance of getting a babysitting job.

So, my dad went with me to get my new puppy. My mom thought it would be good for me to have to get up in the middle of the night to show me how it would be with a baby. Whatever! She thinks up the craziest things. I will show her. I will show that wicked woman I can take care of a dog! I got up with Shasta every night. I taught her how to chase her own tail. I taught her how to roll over. I fed my dog. My mom and dad took me and my dad out to walk almost every night for exercise. Only at night when know one could see me, of course! But I loved my dog. I talked to her about whether or not I should my baby and told my dog all my secrets. Shasta never told anyone not even my mother.

Then I decided to give my baby up for adoption. I knew it was the best for her. Every night I cried myself to sleep. I could not believe God was doing this to me. He broke me and my boyfriend up again, he let me get kicked out of school and now I had to give my baby up for adoption. What type of God would do this to me? God doesn't love me! How could He? He made my own birth mother give me up for adoption and gave me to an adoptive mother that hates me. I am no good and that is why He hates me.

Then why did He make me? Probably because I am really a mistake and am so awful. I hate my life. I wanna die. I wanna kill myself but I am too scared to do it. I am afraid it will hurt. If I could figure out a way to do it without it hurting I would do it. Oh, I can't I am pregnant. Well, after this baby is born I will do it. No! I can not do that either because then I might go to hell and that would really be torture! I already live with the devil herself so why would I kill myself to go live with the real devil for all of eternity. I am in a no win situation. Do not wanna live and do not wanna die. I am stuck!

I will show everyone. I will keep my baby. No! That is not fair to this baby. Why torment this baby because I am unhappy? Maybe I would be happy if I kept the baby?! Then I could move out and get away from everyone. My siblings are mad at me. I have no friends anymore because they all think I am a slut. They're parents will not let them hang around a girl like me. Galatians 6:1-3 says: "Dear brothers and sisters, if another believer is overcome by some sin, you who are godly should gently and humbly help that person back onto the right path. And be careful not to fall into the same temptation yourself. Share each others burdens, and in this way obey the law of Christ. If you think you are too important to help someone you are only fooling yourself. You are not that important."

Where are all these so called christians? They kicked me out of school and turned there backs. I will keep my baby. No! i will have my adoption agent help me find this baby a good home. I will give her to a family that really wants to have a baby and can not.

Then I will not know what she is doing or if this baby gets abused! I heard they do a very thorough background check on families receiving babies. So I believe my agent will find her a safe, loving home. I will ask her at our next appointment.

The agent said I could pick the family through non-identifying information. this means I get to pick the family. I also get to hold the baby in the hospital when it is born. The agent also said I will get pictures of my baby for the first year. Okay. I will give her up. No! I can't. She is mine only. The agency watches over the babies for the first year after placing the baby in a new home. I guess that will be okay. God does not like me so why would He protect my baby? I better keep her. Everyone in my world let me down including God so how can I believe the agent? My mom probably told her to say all these good things to me. Well, God? I know you do not like me will you please watch over my baby if I give her up? It is not this babies fault to be hated by you and everyone else because of me. So God would you at least watch over her?

Forget it. I can not count on God. I will keep her and me and the father can run away and live happily ever after. I do not need anyone.

My water broke. This is not funny. My mom takes me to the hospital. I have an eight pound baby. I am not even fifteen. That was so painful and I am never in life having another baby again.

She is a girl. I name her. I had her four days before my fifteenth birthday. She has tons of black hair. The father comes to see her. He wants us back together to keep her. My sisters come to see her. My whole family comes to see her except my brother. Everyone loves her. I tell my mom I want to keep her. Then I tell my mom, but i can't. i love my baby so much and I want her to have a good life in a family that wants a daughter and will raise her to be a good woman. I can not do that. I am a kid myself. She is beautiful and deserves a beautiful life.

I leave the hospital and my baby has to stay there. She will go to a foster home until she gets to her new adopted home. The agent comes and as soon as I hear the second family from the choices she gives me I know that is the family she needs. She will also have an older brother so I know he will watch over his new little sister. I know this family is going to be a good one, I feel it in my heart. I wrote her a letter on how much I love her and that is why I gave her up because she deserves a life at fifteen that I could not possibly give her. I bought her a ring and a dress.

I went to court and signed off my parental rights. Now she will go to her new family. The agent said the new family will keep the name I gave her. I am so happy about that. I received pictures of her with the ring and dress on that I bought her. She is so cute. I love her. I never knew I could love a person so much.

She is happy. I am not happy. I am happy for her but sad for me. i get back with her father. My parents are furious. We run away. We hitch hike to another city. I made up a new name for myself and say I am eighteen. A guy picks us up and drops us off in the heart of the ghetto in this new city. We are trying to get to Missouri were we heard we could get married even though I was only fifteen. My boyfriend and I get into a huge fight. He beats me up. I hate him now. I want to get away from him. I send him to the store and while he is gone I run as fast as I can down the streets of the ghetto. He is looking for me. A black guy comes out of no where and asks me what is wrong. I tell him I am running away from my boyfriend. The black guy goes down the street and tells my boyfriend I went the opposite way. Then the black guy tells me his name. He says I should go with him and he will take care of me. I go with him. He brings me to a house that has no furniture. It only has a folding table and some chairs in it.

This guy is nice to me. He wants me to be his girlfriend. I tell him I will be. I find out from someone that he is married. He tells me not to believe the person who said he was married. So, I don't. He kisses me. I never kissed a black guy before. It is no different. I leave the house that has no furniture. I keep thinking about the house and how poor they must be. I wonder why people would knock on the door and the ones who knocked would push something through the door and the guys that were in the house would take it and then push something back through the slot in the door. That is wierd.

I see my other black friend. He is a really fast runner. He tells me my boyfriend went back to our home town. I said, good, I am glad he is gone. He asks me if I wanna have a race to see who is the fastest runner. I say, sure. He gives me a huge head start. I lose. He is so fast. Wow!

I tell him about the house with no furniture. He says he already knows. He tells me I am his girlfriend now. I say, okay. We go to the apartment building I was staying at in the ghetto. My new boyfriend and I stay in some guy we just met closet. We have sex. I never had sex with a black guy before. It is no different.

I miss my mom and dad. I want to go home but I can not go back. I want them to come and get me but I can not tell them where I am or they will send the police to come and get me. Besides, I only miss them. I do not wanna live with them. My mom is so crabby and I can not deal with it. She gives me long lectures and half of the time I do not even know what she is talking about. I got good at tuning her out. Whatever. No way can I go back to that but I do not wanna be in the ghetto either.

All the guys around here want to have sex with me. Sick! I have cheap. I try to stay by my boyfriend. He is talking to the other guy who asked me to be his girlfriend first and then we go to the house with no furniture. They must really be poor. There is not even any food. They do have a cot in one of the bedrooms. That was not here before. Oh, they are having a party. they hand me a 40 ounce of beer. I get all buzzed up.

I go lay on the cot. I get up to go find my boyfriend. I hear popping sounds. Everyone jumps down to the ground. i asked them what they are doing down there. I feel my arm being pulled and then I hear someone yell, get down you dumb bitch! They tell me to follow them outside but not to stand up all of the way. I creep out and then start to run. I can hear someone following me. I am scared. I hide but the shadow of the person is coming closer. Oh, it is my boyfriend. It is winter time and i did not even have time to grab my shoes. My toes are so cold. We start to walk to his sisters house.

My feet are totally numb. We go to sleep. I am so tired. The next morning his sister gives me some shoes. I ask him what happened last night. He says the house we were in is a dope house and it was being robbed. I said why did you pull me down to the ground? He said because they were shooting at us. I could not believe I was in a real live dope house being shot at like on tv. That is so cool. Scary, sort of but cool.

We go back to the dope house. My boyfriend shows me where in the wall the bullet holes were. i then realize that if he had not pulled me down to the floor when he did, I would have been shot in the back three times. Now I am scared. My boyfriend says he has to go somewhere so I should stay in the house with no furniture until he comes back in like an hour. three other guys are there and I know them so I agree to stay there and wait for him.

So I am sitting with the guys. I ask if I can push the dope through the slot. They say no. I say why not? I already know it is a dope house I tell them. They just look at each other. This is a normal life to them so for them to meet someone so naive as I was is odd to them. This is normal life.

An hour or so goes by and one of the three black guys tells me he wants to talk to me in the other room. I go in the other room with him. He wants to have sex. I say no! He grabs me and starts kissing my neck. I tell him to stop. He tells me to shut up! I push him away and he grabs me and pushes me to the floor. He punches me. He is six feet tall and about 250 pounds. I feel him grab my head and he starts to pound it into the ground. I feel blood. He rapes me. I am so dizzy. I wanna leave. I run for the door and he hits me in the eye. I refused to let myself cry. I would not give him that much satisfaction. I try to open the door but can not open it. It is still all boarded up from the robbery. I ask for help. Another guy about 5'6 and 175 pounds grabs me. He pulls me into the other bedroom. He pushes me to the ground and rapes me too. He keeps talking while he rapes me but I am tuning him out. I am so good at that because of my mothers long lectures. I think my nose is broken. Blood is all over. I am getting mad. Very Mad. I yell any of you other pigs want some? I remember there is only one other guy in the house so if worse came to worse there would only be one more.

I get to the door. The guy opens it for me. I run. I run right to the apartment complex I was staying at, I walk in. A white guy that lives there sees me. He starts asking me what happened. He starts to clean up the blood on my face. It does not seen to him that anything is broken. I tell him what happened. He tells me he will take me to a clinic tomorrow. He thinks I should get checked for STD's. I say, okay. I go and take a shower and then I cry. I feel so gross. I want my mom. I wanna go home.

A lady in the building comes to talk to me. Mark told her. She tells me it is not my fault. They had no right to rape me or make me do anything I did not want to do. She is so nice. She tells me I should tell my parents where I am so they can come and get me. I tell her maybe. My ex-boyfriend that I had came to this city with already told the police where I was. I am considered a runaway because I am only really sixteen. The police find me. They take me back to the city I came from. I am glad deep down. I want my mom. The big city cops had questioned me and made me feel like I was a slut and wanted to know things that I did not know. They told me I had been around very dangerous people. I told them I had been raped and they acted like I was lying. They said the area I had been living in the past month is so dangerous even they get nervous going into that area. I remember asking God to help me. I said to God, even though you do not like me please protect me and keep me safe. He did not keep me safe. I was brutally raped.

My mom and sister said I look thin and tired. I thought I looked good. I told them what happened. Two months later I found out I was pregnant. I knew it could very well be from the rape. I also knew there was a possibility it was from my first babies father. I did not care. I am not and will not give this baby up for adoption. Sh

I start getting things ready for this babies birth. I tell my parents I am keeping the baby. They simply say, okay it is my decision. What? Okay? Is this a trick? You mean no long dragged out lecture? Just okay? Maybe they feel this baby belongs in our family. Maybe they love it as much as I do already? I do not care if it is from the rape I tell them. They still say, okay. This is weird. My mom always made my decisions. Not this time. I will fight for this baby no matter what.

I am in labor. Dang, this hurts. I thought I said I was not having anymore kids after the last painful birth. Dang this hurts.

My baby is born. She is a girl. She has tons of black hair. She is beautiful. I love her. She is dark. Good! I am happy. That means she is not from the first babies father. Thank goodness. I do not want to be tied to him for eighteen plus years. The nurse asks me what her name will be. I tell her. I give her the same name as the nice lady that talked to me after I had been raped. She was exactly what I needed after that experience. I give her the name of a lady I consider an angel. God sent her to me, to cry with me, to comfort me.

As the months go by I feel so connected to this baby. I feel like we have been through so much together already. I hear my mom on the phone telling someone I did keep this baby and telling the person no, she has feelings against abortion. She knows God does not make mistakes and this baby is meant to be here. Wow! She actually stuck up for me. Unbelievable. Some people ask me why would I keep a baby that is from a rape? My response even though I was still mad at God was, What are the chances of my getting pregnant from one incident? Very slim so she is part of God's plan, whatever it may be. Jeremiah 1:5 says: "I knew you before I formed you in your mother's womb. Before you were born I set you apart and appointed you as my prophet to the nations".

So there you have it. He knew what he was doing and that is why we call Him, God!

She is part of His ultimate plan. She is here for a reason and a purpose. I believe something good always comes out of something bad. She is my good out of that bad. I would go through it all over again for her! She was so worth it!

I meet a guy. He is Native American. He is so cute. We start seeing each other. After going together for a while we plan to run away and get married. We set it up at the courthouse. I will not be leaving town this time after what happened to me last time I ran away. So we only run away to get married in town. We did it. We got married. My parents do not know. I feel free. No more having to deal with my mother. We live on the reservation at his mothers apartment. We have my daughter with us. We have to stay at his mothers for a while. I am a barber student and he does not have a job. We have no money and no where else to go. We never thought we may need an apartment or jobs. I am only eighteen and he is nineteen.

We get an apartment down the hall from his mothers apartment. I am still on AFDC and food stamps so that is what we live on. My dad drives all the way to the reservation from the city to take me to school and drop off my daughter at the babysitters.

My new husband of a month becomes abusive towards me. I am asleep on the couch and I feel a forceful punch on my head. I sit up. I feel something warm running down the back of my neck. It is blood. I ask him why he did that. He says it was because he wants me to wake up. I think to myself don't people just say, "wake up"? Obviously not him. I feel dizzy. I call my mom and she comes to pick up my daughter. I stay at the apartment with my husband. I have school the next day. I am so tired. My head really hurts. I go to sleep but am afraid he is going to hit me again so I barely sleep.

My dad comes to get me for school the next morning. I show him my bloody shirt. I skip school and he takes me to the doctor. My head was cut open by his punch but I do not need stitches. The doctor does a pregnancy test. It is positive. It is my third child and I am only eighteen years old. While I was pregnant with my second daughter I had managed to get my GED. I knew the importance of education and knew that would be a ticket to freedom. That is why I began the technical school for barbering to be independant and provide for my kids. Somehow I manage to keep it together but it is hard with a new abusive husband, a year old baby, going to school full-time and pregnant. I want my mom. Why do i keep thinking this? Am I not the very person who claims she is so evil and the one I am trying to get away from? Even though I do not admit it, I love her and need her desperately.

After my pregnancy test I go to my moms. I will spend the night over there. I get my daughter from the babysitters. I call my sister-in-law to tell my husband I am sleeping at my moms. She has to tell him because we do not have a phone. That is part of life on welfare. I guess. This is why I need an education so I can get a good job and have even the simple things like a phone. I go to sleep. I am totally worn out.

I go back to our apartment on the reservation. I leave my daughter at my parents. My husband and I get along. He says he is sorry for punching me in the head and promises never to do it again. I believe him. He sounds sincere.

A couple days later we have another fight. He chokes me and I pass out. Why would he do that and he knows I am pregnant? I am leaving and moving back to my moms. I can not let him away at know or he will try and stop me or beat me up again. I have to try and sneak away. He pushes me and tells me he is going to kill himself. I said, good. Go get your gun and shoot yourself in the head! You are always cutting your wrists so stop playing around and shoot yourself! I did not mean what I was saying. I am just mad.

I go to my parent's house again after school. I have my my daughter. I am asleep in my older sister's room, she is away at college. It is two in the morning and both of my parents are sitting on the bed telling me to wake up. What, no punch in the head to wake me up? How nice. Then I realize it is the middle of the night and I ask my parents what is wrong? Is it my daughter? They say no, she is fine. They then tell me my husband is in the hospital with a gun shot wound. I automatically think it is due to hunting. He is always hunting deer out of season and so I think he accidently shot himself in the leg or something. I think to myself how clumsy!

I get to the hospital. His mom is in the waiting room and crying. Why is she crying, I wonder. Something is wrong. At eleven o'clock last night he had called to tell me he was going to kill himself. I had said, good and hung up. Did he really do it? no, he could have! The doctor comes out to talk to me. My mom is with me. My dad is home watching over my daughter. The doctor says he is on a respirator and it is keeping him alive. He is brain dead due to a gun shot wound to the head. He is going to die anytime now. I can not believe this doctor just said that. I ask to see him. I am in shock. This can not be true. i need to see for myself.

I go into his room. He looks like he is asleep. There is a bandage between his eyebrows. The doctor said that is where he shot himself. Between the eyebrows with a shot gun called a 22. He could not hear me and he could not see me. His brain was totally scrambled. They say once a 22 hits its target the bullet shatters inside of whatever it hits. That is what happen here. It shattered his brain. I need to get out of his room. I leave and go to the waiting room. Out of no where it seems a pastor from the church on the reservation is there. No one even called him. He just showed up but how did he know? Weird. The nurse comes into the waiting room and tells us my husband is about to die and is in his last few minutes. She tells us we can go in and spend the last few minutes with him if we would like. I say no, I can not go in there while he dies. I have never seen death before.

I am scared. I tell my mom to go in there and she does. She is gone thirty seconds and I ask the pastor to go in there with me and he does. I watch as the respirator shuts down. He is dead. My husband has just died from suicide. I lose it. I began to cry like I have never cried in my life. Is this a dream? Am I still asleep? No, this is real. Why? Why did this happen? I am in shock, I am hurt, I am angry. Does God really hate me this much? Doesn't He ever want me happy? I am pregnant! Maybe he isn't really dead. I ask my mom to jiggle him and see if he is really dead. He is. It is true. I leave the room. I can not stop crying. My heart feels like it split. I feel guilt suddenly. I told him to do it! Oh my gosh!

I did not mean it! I was mad. God please bring him back! Please! We can work it out! It is too late. This hurts more than anything I have been through.

His baby will never get to meet him. This baby will grow up without a father.

Then I think about when I had met him. I was doing volunteer work at a mental health hospital visiting a lady now and then. To get to her ward I would have to walk through the juvenile ward. It was then that I saw a tall dark handsome native. He was there for suicide attempts. He had slit his wrists on numerous occasions. He tells me to call him because he goes home tomorrow. The next day I call him. That is how we got together.

I knew nothing about suicide. I was eighteen and he was nineteen when he died. We were married two months and I was only two months pregnant. Now that I am older and wiser I see his suicide signs and the events that lead up to it. I look back and see his depression. Rapid weight loss, negative statements, lack of interest in things he liked to do and most of the all his attempts at suicide before the actual death. I felt guilty for a long time because of what I had said to him. Along, long time.

During the funeral arrangements I was numb. I answered questions and continued to care for my one year old daughter but barely remember the funeral. I was there physically but not mentally.

My parents suggested I go to counseling. No way! Counseling for what? I do not need counseling! I failed to realize I had been a survivor of molestation, survivor of a brutal rape, was adopted, gave a baby up for adoption, had three kids before was a victim of domestic violence and now a widow all before the age of eighteen and I do not need counseling? I had been through more in my short life than most people go through in an entire life. No, definately no need for counseling was my answer.

I had my new baby. She is so cute and looks just like her dad. I love that she looks like him. She is my present that he left me. A life long present.

I meet another Native American. I like the fact that he is Native like my husband was. Almost immediately after meeting him I get an apartment and he moves in with me. Not long after he moved in my mom said my older daughter tells her that my new boyfriend is touching her butt. My mom says she believes he is molesting her. I am mad but not mad at him. I am mad my mom would make up such an evil lie. He would never do that. She is barely two years old but I ask her if he is touching her. She just looks at me blankly. She never said that to me so my mom must be lying. But that blank look she gave me makes me worry. I never saw her look like that before. No, my mom must be brainwashing her. My mom has social workers come to talk to me. The leave me a paper with signs to watch for just in case he is touching her. I still do not believe it. I read the signs anyway.

My youngest is now about nine months old. She shares a bedroom with my near two year old. Why is he in their bedroom? He won't let me come in. I can see through the crack in the door. Do I go in and let him be mad and beat me up or do I just stay out? What if he is molesting my daughters? My oldest daughter sees me and I know something is wrong. i decide to go in and take the beating. Anything to protect my daughters. I go in and he yells for me to get out. I yell no back to him. He comes after me. So what! At least he is not hurting my kids. He beats me up. The good looking native with long hair, perfect teeth and funny sense of humor is a monster. A child molestor. Am I sure? I have to be sure he is really a molestor. I will call the social workers tomorrow and ask them to come over. I need to know what they think.

My daughters are playing on the floor. My oldest does some odd things. She does something that totally convinces me she has been molested. Possibly my other daughter also. I feel fire go through my head. I am mad. I want to kill him. I guess I won't need to call the social workers. I believe my mom.

How could this happen? What type of God lets this happen to little children? I know God hates me but why torture my children? Doesn't it say in His very own bible not to hurt His little children? Yet he has allowed this monster to hrt hurt mine!

I start to drink. I start to drink alot. I have already kicked the molestor out of my house. I told him I would kill him. One day when he is not expecting it, I will get him, torture him and kill him. I say this with a knife in my hand. He was walking out when I threw the knife in an attempt to hit him in the back. He closed the door and it stuck in the door where he had been. Damn! I missed. Next time!

The pain of knowing he hurt my babies was unbearable. i feel pure hate. I never thought I could hat another person until this man hurt my children.

I have failed at everything in my life and now I have failed as a mother. I do not deserve these precious babies. I have let them down just like I do everyone and everything in my life. I am mad at God more now than ever before. My heart is becoming hard. I ask God, why? I tell him he can do whatever he wants to me but to let my children get hurt is another story. I begin to turn from a sweet naive girl to a monster.

I drink even more. I do not like to drink but it takes away the pain. My kids are staying with my parents more and more. The pain does not go away. It never dawned on me now would be the perfect time to go to counseling. Beer is my counselor. Eventually my parents are the sole caregivers for my daughters. I go to my parents house to visit whenever I can manage to get sober enough. Everyday I think about killing the man who molested my daughters.

I see the molestor's car. I smash the window. I get a criminal damage fine. I do not care. He is lucky that was all it was. I go to his house. I smash his parents window. I get put on probation. I still drink. I have to drink. I need to stop this pain I feel for letting my kids down.

I go to the bar. I am with two very large natives. My best friends. We see the molestor. Today is the day I get my revenge. Today he will die for hurting my kids. My friends want him to suffer just as much as I do.

I go up to the molestor and pretend like I am not mad. I pretend like everything is okay. I buy him a beer. We all just talk and drink except I slow way down on my drinking because I need to have this be the day I get my revenge. We go to another bar. My friend has a van. The molestor sits in the front passenger seat. I sit in back with my other big friend. I tell my friend, NOW! He grabs the molestor around the neck until he passes out. My other friend stops the van. I jump out. We are in an alley. I pull the molestor out of the van. He hits the ground. I start stomping on his head. I punch him. I stomp on him. I stomp on him again. I stomp on him again and again and again. I can not stop! All the anger I had bottled up over the year since I saw him last is coming out. Blood is everywhere. My friends yell for me to stop. I can't. I want him dead. I want him to suffer like he made my daughters suffer. No matter how much counseling my daughters get, my beautiful daughters will never forget what he did to them. If this molestor lives I want this to be one beating he will never forget.

We start to leave. I look back at him and spit on him. Then I run back and jump on his pelvis area. My friends can not believe I just beat a man twice my size. I explain to my friends it was pure hate that allowed me to beat a man twice my size. My friends told me do not be suprised if you are arrested. I say I do not care. I tell them sitting life in prison to stick up for my children. I am full of blood. I go home.

My room-mate tells me the police were here looking for me. Wow! That was fast. It must be serious. Good. I am ready.

The next day I go to my mom's house to see my daughters. My mom tells me the police had been there last night looking for me. I turn around and see the police at the front door. I go outside and they arrest me. I ask what are my charges? They tell me it is for "strong-armed robbery and battery". I say, what? You mean it is not murder? It should have been murder I tell the arresting officer. On the way to jail I tell him why I did what I did to the molestor. He tells me he can understand my anger because he has kids too but that doesn't give me the right to try and kill him. I ask him how did I get a robbery charge too? Apparently my friend stoled his wallet when it fell out of his pocket. I was mad. I was mad because my charge was murder and that meant he could hurt more kids.

The judge would not let me out of jail on bond since I was being held on a probation violation anyway. I was on probation for criminal damage to property. I had to stay in jail until my next court date.

I hated jail. I talked to God even though I still believed He hated me. I cried every night because I missed my kids so much. I wanted my kids to know that I loved them so much I would kill for them. I wanted them to know that even though I did not believe my mom at first and had not protected them that I was sorry and I loved them. in my sick way of thinking I believed this would prove that I loved them. It never dawned on me that my absence from being in jail would only add more hurt and pain on top of the hurt and pain they already went and are still going through.

The molestor was arrested and convicted for sexually molesting my children. He is currently a registered sex offender. He will have to live with this his whole life just as my daughters will. The difference is, my daughters are strong and resilient while the molestor is weak and marked for life like the "beast" he is.

My daughters remained with my parents. I was sentenced to two years in prison. During my prison stay nothing inside me changed. I thought about getting out and killing him. I needed counseling but at the time didn't believe I did. I was at my highest peak of anger at God. I was becoming more and more unreachable. But even though i thought God did not like me I still asked him to please watch over my daughters and keep them safe, happy and healthy.

In prison I was housed with some very dangerous criminals. Some were serving life sentences and called "lifers".

Some had killed their own children, some were child molestors. One girl killed her own mother and another killed her baby and fed it to her husband because she was mad at him. Others were there for prostitution, drugs, forgery or petty thefts. No matter what they were serving time for the thing about all of them was they looked and seemed like everyday people. They even think of themselves as an everyday person but society considers them notorious.

I had met an older lady who seemed so nice. I later found out she was in prison for running a child pornography ring. I could not believe it! She looked like someone's grandmother and probably is but thankfully not my grandmother!

It also amazed me at the amount of lesbianism that goes on inside prison. I am not talking about a truly lesbian woman. I am talking about being what they call "gay for the stay". That means you are gay while you are incarcerated. You liked men when you came into prison and you will go back to men once released but while they are in prison they have “girlfriends”. Some actually kiss their girlfriend good-bye on their way to a visit to see their husband and children. Most times the prison guards do their best to separate the girlfriends and put them in different buildings. This only makes watching how they maintain their relationships all more amusing. They maintain their relationships by yelling “I love you” to each other through two baseball fields, passing notes they call “dyke kites” to each other and through other people. They will do anything to get five minutes just to walk to a meal with their girlfriend. Although they are very creative I wonder if they put this much effort into maintaining relationships with their children. I wonder.

Prison is a world by itself. Some talk as though they deserve better food which is actually pretty good. Some talk as if rules should not apply to them only to others. Some act as though they are in an up-scale hotel. Some of these women forget they lived in roach infested apartments before prison if they had an apartment at all.

Oh and what an exciting day it is when we have bananas or hotdogs. They call this "ladies night". Or they act like nine year old boys holding the banana in front of their pants or saying sexual comments about what they could do with that hotdog. Some of the mentalities behind that fence are unbelieveable.

I was totally shocked one day when one woman told another woman to shut up because the woman responded by saying, you do not tell me to shut up you tell your kids to shut up! I thought to myself I would never tell me kids to shut up. I would only tell a dog to shut up or a woman that meant nothing to me! Never a child!

I was talking to some women who considered themselves husslers. They are the ones who go from person to person trying to get what they can from whomever they can. So, I asked them what was the difference between a hussler and a beggar? They said there is a big difference. I asked, what? They could not answer me. That is because there is no difference. They refer to themselves as husslers because then it does not seem so bad when actually it is begging. Or the word player. A woman that acts like a man (or boy) is called a stud. So many of the studs refer to themselves as players because they have several girlfriends usually one in each building. (easier to keep them from finding each other out) These are women who act like boys an even though they call themselves players they are still hoes. If they do this in here they are worse on the street. Worse hoe or worse player? Oh, thats right it is the same thing.

Speaking of hoes, the best justification I have heard yet is, I am not a hoe, I am an escort! Calling themselves escorts is better than calling themselves a hoe. I again, asked what the difference was. Being an escort is not the same as a hoe because they get paid big money. Hoes get pennies. I also asked the ones with husbands and boyfriends isn't it considered cheating if you are escorting? Their reply was, no, they are getting paid! So, if they were not getting paid then they would be cheating? Whether it is beggar, hustler, player or hoe it is all the same thing. They simply label it different to make it more acceptable in their mind. It makes it easier for them to live with themselves because they know deep down it is wrong! Like the saying goes, "I want what I want when I want it with no regards for anyone else, only self".

To get my mind healthier in this type of setting would be difficult. So, I focused on the other side of this. For instance, the amount of talent behind the fence is amazing! I heard some of the most amazing singers, saw beautiful art work, excellent dancers and funny comedians. I had some good laughs with some women that had unspeakable crimes. I saw them pull together and make huge ordeals for other people's birthday's. They did for mine. I sometimes wondered what happened? Were they abused as children? Were they victims of the system? Were they raped? What made some of these women do what they did? Anger and hate like me? I am sure some were raised in loving homes like I was but what really happened?

My mind really got to thinking about how I got there. Oh, I knew how I got there. I tried to kill a man who molested my children but not everyone responds the way I did. So, how did I really get here? Chemical imbalance? Or simply my own bad decisions? Biological make-up? Or all of it put together? Doesn't matter right now, I am still out to get the molestor.

I did almost a year in prison and went to a half-way house. I did almost a year and start talking to God again. I asked him how could He turn His back on me? When I needed Him, He was not there. For the first time in the three months at the half-way house I saw the poem on the wall that had been there all along-FOOTPRINTS.

One night I had a dream. I dreamed I was walking along the beach with the Lord. Across the sky flashed scenes from my life. For each scene, I noticed two sets of footprints in the sand: one belonging to me, and the other to the Lord.

When the last scene of my life flashed before me, I looked back to the footprints in the sand. I noticed that many times along the path of my life there were only one set of footprints. I also noticed that it happened at the lowest and saddest times in my life.

This really bothered me and I questioned the Lord about it. "Lord, you said that once I decided to follow you, you'd walk with me all the way. But I have noticed that during the most troublesome times in my life, there is only one set of footprints. I don't un-

> derstand why when I needed you most you would leave me.
>
> The Lord replied, "My precious, precious child. I love you and would never leave you. During your times of trial and suffering, when you see only one set of footprints, it was then that I carried you.

This really got me thinking. Is He really carrying me? Is He really carrying my daughters? Are all these things happening because of my own choices and decisions? Do I really need counseling? Am I crazy?

I need to change my life. I decided I would move to a brand new city and start all over. I would get my daughters from my parents house and live happily ever after. I did not know that unless I dealt with my issues and got help a geographical change would not make a difference. No matter where I went I would always still be right there so until I dealt with myself nothing would change.

So I moved to the new town, I found a job waitressing and started dating the cook. I worked about 60 hour weeks and loved the restaurant business. I was really doing well. Still no counseling. I am doing well anyway so really there is no need for counseling look how good I am doing. It would be and was only a matter of time.

My new boyfriend is black. You would think after being raped by two black guys I would never date a black guy. Even I was not that ignorant. I would not hate the whole african a american race because of those two losers. So instantly I let him move in with me. He did not know that I had already been introduced to crack cocaine. I had only did it a few times. I don't really count that it was only a few times. I was still in pain so of course I tried a new drug.

I kept my double life secret from my boyfriend. I had sugar-daddies. I would sneak around when my boyfriend was at work. He hated drugs. I did not smoke crack everyday. I was a binger. I would get high then not do it again for sometimes years at a time but when I did I spent everything I had saved. I would purposely start an argument to have an excuse to run off and get high. I would stay high about three to five days at a time until my body couldn't take anymore. Obviously, by this time my boyfriend new what I was doing.

I learned how to lie better. Con better. Manipulate better. I told people what they wanted to hear especially men. I was becoming my surroundings and becoming more and more like the people I associated with. Well, of course I was. No one descent would want to be around a dope-feen and that is what I was. I justified it by saying I was only a binger.

Like that makes a difference.

I am an alcoholic and a dope-feen. It took away the pain of my life and current lifestyle.

My plan to do better was not working. I did however talk to God more. I would be going to the dope house asking God to keep me safe. After all I was paranoid. Crack causes extreme paranoia. My friends that were good friends turned their backs on me when they found out I wasn't what I seemed to be. I did not look like a dope-feen. I was very pretty at this age, tan, thin and definately fooled alot of people about what I really was. My looks helped me manipulate. Even my dope-feen friends were turning on me. They did not want me around their boyfriends. Their boyfriends didn't mind. I was low down and nasty to many people. I had become a good fighter and would fight in an instant. I had credit for crack with one of the biggest dope dealers in the city I was living in. I wonder how many cars I bought him. I should say, I wonder how many cars my sugar-daddies bought him. This went on for about four years.

My boyfriend and I got married. He was an alcoholic. A hard-core alcoholic. He had a soft nature about him. The most attractive feature he had was his beautiful smile. The best coo I had ever seen. Everyone wanted him as the cook for there restaurant. He was the best. However, he did get fired alot for throwing temper-tantrums due to his drinking. The employer always seemed to tolerate his drinking before and during work because he was just that good and fast. Until, the temper-tantrum and then he would get fired but usually hired again. By the same employer. He was a Christian. He had one son he loved dearly but could not give him his all because of his alcoholism. Alcoholism and drug addictions only let you go so far in relationships, go so far in life and will never let a person reach their full potential. Alcoholism is a cunning, baffling disease. It will turn a good person into the opposite. My new husband's sense of humor was great. I came from a family with excellent sense of humors so this was important to me. We eventually moved back to the town my daughters lived in. Away from the crack.

I am clean and sober again. My alcoholic husband would have to drink a half pint of vodka just to get up strength for work. This six foot black man was never afraid to cry. Anytime, any place, if he felt the need to cry he would do just that.

We still laugh at how sensitive he was and how he would just cry in front of anyone. One day at a job interview he cried during the interview and when he came out to the car in tears I thought he had blown it. Nope! He was to start the next day. Unbelievable. The truth is this man was in pain. I never could figure out why he would not or could not quit. He didn't like to be mean to people yet he was because of his drinking. He loved his family yet could not show it because of his drinking. He had so much to give yet couldn't because of his drinking. I had now been clean and sober for several years and couldn't stand living the life of an alcoholic when I was clean and worked so hard not too live like this. I filed for divorce.

I told him to get help. If he got sober I would not divorce him. He got help but immediately drank again. I wanted him but that was impossible while he was still drinking. I wish I could have divorced the alcoholic part and kept him but we know that is not the way it works.

This divorce pushed him over the edge. I was his world and I turned my back on him. I was the one he could count on and I left.

After we divorced I started drinking. How could I do the very same thing I divorced him for? This does not make sense. I was going down fast. Even though a person gets sober the second they go back to drinking they go back to exactly where they left off before they got sober and each time it gets worse. So it wasn't long before I lost a good job for not showing up because I was drunk or hung over. It didn't take long to lose family trust, to lose my nice duplex, fight with friends over money, get several drunk drivings and be back in debt. The farther I went down the more depressed I became the more I drank. Still no counseling.

I was finally court-ordered to participate in a six month hard-core extensive treatment program by the State of Wisconsin. It was the roughest experience I ever had. I had to talk about feelings. I had to tell my story. I had to cry until I could cry no more. I had to apologize to people I had embarrassed and hurt. I had to tell my sister who has a high position within the courts that I was sorry for embarrassing her. I had to read a letter to my group from my other sister about she felt like she did not even know me anymore. That it felt like I was a shell of a person she once knew. I had to read letters from my own daughters telling me how my drinking affected them. i heard my daughter tell me now when I was drunk I had told her how I wished I would have had an abortion instead of having her. Oh my gosh! I never meant that! I still can not believe I had said that! What type of mother says that to their own daughter. A very sick type and that is what I was. I had to hear my other daughter tell me how I had pushed and hit her when I was drunk. I never did hear from my brother. He is so hurt by my actions he can not even stand to be in the same room as me. Hearing all this, talking about all this, crying and getting mad over all this, was the best thing that has ever happened to me. It didn't feel like the best at the time but it was the beginning of a life changing experience.

I found my relationship with God, again. The poem, "Footprints in the Sand" is oh so true. It WAS then that He carried me through. He wasn't just carrying me but He was carrying my daughters and my whole family too! The Lord had never left me at all!

Joshua 1:5 says: "I will never leave you nor forsake you."

Are you kidding me? He was with me all along? He was listening to my cries and protecting my children? Thank you, Jesus!

I know the Lord has a purpose and a plan for my life. I do not know what His purpose or plan is but through all of this, I do not have a scratch on me. Not a scrape, not a scratch! I have been in roach infested apartments with dopefeens and dealers with guns. Yet, not a bruise, not a mark. That was all God. He not only took care of my children when I couldn't and wouldn't, but He took care of me too!

Psalm 20:1 says: "In times of trouble, may the Lord answer your cry. May the name of the God of Jacob keep you safe from harm."

Isaiah 46:4 says: "I will be your God throughout your life time-until your hair is white with age. I made you, and I will care for you. I will carry you along and save you."

Oh, I am not perfect. I will never be that. I still think people are out to get me at times, I am forgetful and get frustrated easily. I do not learn as quickly as I used to but besides this, I am in one piece or should I say, one "peace". Some people ask me if I could change one thing in my life what would it be. The only thing I would change is the hurt and pain I have caused my family. I would not change anything else.

I went through and made the choices I made, maybe because God allowed it so I could help another person. He could have intervened at anytime and changed the direction of my life but He did not do that. Why didn't He?

Phillippians 1:29 says: "Is there any chance, any possibility that you have been selected to struggle for God's glory? Have you "been granted for Christ's sake, not only to believe in Him, but also to suffer for His sake?"

What about the story of the blind man? He was selected by God so the works of God maybe displayed in Him.

A month before treatment was over the director told me I needed to stay another month. It was a six month program and he told me I needed to stay a seventh month. What? Is he crazy? I do not need another month. Obviously, I did. Not only to get my head truly together but I also believe God kept me away another month because of other things He was doing. I was still frustrated because I had other things planned.

Proverbs 16:33 says: "We may throw the dice, but the Lord determines how they fall".

So fine, another month what can I really do about it anyway. I had planned on getting back together with my second husband. My still active in his alcoholism ex-husband. Two weeks before I was to finish my seventh month of treatment the director called me into his office again. I thought, oh great another month. No. He told me my ex-husband was found dead in a motel room. He had a high blood pressure and wouldn't take his pills because you can not drink on blood pressure pills. So instead of not drinking he didn't take the pills. Typical alcoholic choice. Five years prior to his death they had told him to stop drinking or he would be dead in three years. He knew his kidneys were barely holding it together but alcohol always won.

When that director told me he was dead due to his alcoholism my heart broke again. I believe God kept me in treatment that extra month to keep me out of way and to protect me from possibly drinking over his death. I think about him everyday. Anyone who knows anything about the death of an alcoholic knows it is not a pretty sight. I still to this day can not believe he is dead. I have no one to call me at three in the morning talking drunk nonsense babble to me. I miss him deeply. He was an incredible man, an awesome cook but alcohol won.

With my extensive treatment and my ex-husband's death and my decision to become different and better, I see the transformation that God is doing within me and for my life. I am totally different than what I was.

I know my birth mother was only sixteen when she decided to give me up for adoption. I know how hard that decision was for her. I would like to meet her one day but most of all I would love to meet my birthfather. He didn't know she was giving me up for adoption. He was at home waiting for her to return with me. She returned but not with me so I feel as though he has a broken heart. I need to meet my birthfather not just for me but for him as well.

Getting raped at sixteen by those men I am not angry. I am grateful. I got the ultimate reward for the pain I went through. I have my daughter. She must also realize that she is also here for a reason. God has a plan for her life. God could have not allowed me to get pregnant from that rape but He did allow it. He does not ever make mistakes. She is meant to be here. We are all made in his image! What a blessing it is to have her in my life.

My first husbands suicide saddens me because my daughter will never get to meet her dad. I consider her the present he left me. Now that is one heck of a present! I never understood why God let him commit suicide. God is All-Powerful and could have intervened and stopped him from killing himself. But He didn't. I now believe it was meant to happen that way. It was meant to happen just like that, at that time. What is the reason and purpose for letting a nineteen year old boy die? We may never know the reasoning or what God's plan is in this or the reason why,- He works in mysterious ways.

If you reading this book are thinking about committing suicide, DO NOT DO IT!!! Pain is temporary. Death is permanent! Talk to someone. Get help. Call your local Crisis Center. It hurts to talk about painful experiences but you must do it in order to feel better. In order to get better. Cry, scream stomp around but do not take your own life. There is no coming back. No changing your mind. You are also here for a reason. You ARE part of God's plan. If you have attempted suicide and not succeeded what does that say? God is not ready for you yet! He has a plan and purpose for you right here! So no matter how many times you try if He is not ready, you are staying right here! It is in His time so you may as well work through your pain and see what God has in store for you!

I once read a book about a girl who had been raped. She became so depressed that she jumped in front of a train. Fifty-five freight cars went over her and as she was being sucked under by the force of the train, another force was pulling her another direction. Her legs were severed by the train and she lived. Now that was God intervening and not allowing he to die. He had a plan for that incident. Today she talks to people about suicide, depression and helps people all over the world. She is a miracle. It showed me something.

It showed me that God could have jammed my first husband's gun and He did not do that. It was meant to be and that is why I let go of the guilt I felt for saying what I said to him days before he died. Whether I would have said it or not, he was going to die.

Suicide is a selfish way to go. Yes it is. The person only things about their own pain and not so much about the effect their death will have on the people who love them. That is actually normal. When a person is so depressed and so sad it hurts so bad that all you can see is your own pain. A depressed person doesn't mean to be selfish they actually think they are doing everyone a favor. It has a person thinking that way. It often absorbs you so much you can not get help yourself, or you think you can handle it on your own (which you obviously can not or you would not be thinking about or trying suicide) or you can not get yourself on medications to help. If you know anyone thinking about this, try to get them help. Even if they say they do not want help get it regardless. If need be, call the police. Let them assess the situation. Yes, you may feel guilty but this guilt is nothing compared to the guilt you will feel if you do not try to help them and they succeed. Always take suicidal threats serious! God may be using you to save a life!

As for the molestor of my daughters, I forgive him. He is very sick but I had to forgive in order to get well. He was not my daughters only abuser. I was too. I walked out on my daughters when they needed me most. When my daughters needed me to hug them and tell them it would be okay, I wasn't there.

I was so absorbed in my own poor me type thinking that I walked out. I left them at their grandparents house and began a life of alcohol, drugs and a chaotic lifestyle. Instead of being a caring, loving, nurturing mother, I turned into a cold, selfish person with no regards for anyone but myself. Like the saying goes, "hurt people hurt people" and my hurt led me into hurting every single person I came into contact with.

Now through counseling, many prayers from my parents especially my mother and God's love, I am back to myself! I care for people and their feelings so much now I can not believe I do some of the things I do for some. I do my best to treat everyone fairly and with respect even if I do not want too. Who am I to treat God's creations badly! To me that is like saying, what God created is not good enough for me! Like I know better than Him! So, I do my best to be nice to everyone no matter what!

I see some of the people I drank with in my twenties and hear them tell me how I used to be. I was mean. I was awful. I look at them and I thank God He carried me through. There is still hope for them. No matter how bad an alcoholic or drug addict, there is always hope. I will always be there for a fellow alcoholic or drug addict. I will however be careful not to fall back into that type of lifestyle and always have my guard up to keep myself safe. I will take someone with me because there is always a chance I could slip and I will always be there for the alcoholic that still suffers.

So, yes! I forgive the molestor. I am still disgusted and sickened by it because those were my children. I also remember Romans 2:6 says: "He will judge everyone according to what they have done". He also says "vengeance is mine, saith the Lord". So he can hold himself accountable for his actions. He can explain to the Lord why he molested my daughters. He can deal with the Lord on judgement day! He will never have control over my actions or decisions again. I take back my kids and my control. Knowing he will deal with the All-Powerful One, allowed me to forgive, cope and have my life back.

My prison experience was good for me. I consider it a test. Do I let myself become my surroundings or do I let my Christian morals, values and teachings come through? Even though at this time I still had not totally gone back to him yet, I still had Him in me. When you teach a little child something over and over, they may stray away but it is still in them and always will be. Whether or not they choose to acknowledge it is another thing. Sort of like the "prodigal son". He ran off and left his family to get wild. When he was ready to "get right" he went back to what he knew and what he was! Like my parents, his father loved him regardless of the things he had done. He still loved him and waited for him to return and he did. I did too. My parents heart broke when they watched me become exactly what they told me not to become. They watched with tears in their eyes as I became the person they warned me about and they still love me unconditionally.

Not everyone has parents and a family like I was blessed with and that is totally okay. If you are going through things please get help and work through it. If you are too afraid to ask for help still get it out. Tell your cat, a bird in the park or go to an open field and yell and scream and just get it all out. Then do it again the next day, the day after that and the day after that-just get it out! If you don't, you will self-destruct. It will come out in self-destructive behaviors such as alcoholism, drug addiction, gambling, sexual acts, violence or whatever! It will come out somehow, someway! A person has to talk in order to get better and feel better, plain and simple. You do not need a good family or good people around to get well. It helps, but it is not necessary. If everyone around you is just as messed up, get a pillow and beat it up! Get your anger out, cry your tears and as you get healthier you will find good people who care.

The most amazing thing is, God is always there to listen. You can yell, you can yell at Him. You can swear, you can swear at Him. Your prayers do not have to be perfect. He knows your heart, what you are thinking and what you plan to say even before you say it. So keep it real, He knows anyway. He understands and that is why He had His son die on the cross for us. Be- we are human.

For anyone who wants nothing to do with God that is your choice. But why not try it? What do you have to lose? Nothing! You will never know what He can do in your life unless you try. It does not matter if you are a drunk, prostitute, murderer or even a child molestor because He will forgive you, if you ask.

If you do not want to try God and see what He can do for you, then still get help. Whether you believe or not, I do and I know that you are His child and He will send someone to help you.

I am not anywhere close to where I should be in life but I am no where close to where I used to be. I am a survivor! I am a miracle! No problem is too big for God! So tell Him! For the non-believer, then tell someone else but God is listening to you even if you are not talking to Him and even if you do not believe in Him He believes in you!

I have spoken to teens about choices and decisions in the past. Whether or not you turn to God wouldn't you rather be safe than sorry? But if you are not willing to try Him out then get an education. That is your ticket out of any situation. You do not have to be super smart or rich to go to college. Do your best in school and talk to your teachers for help to get into college and you have unbelieveable power to do and go anywhere. I promise it is the secret, the ticket to anywhere.

My opinion of alcohol and drugs are the devil in disguise. The saying, conning and baffling always gave me the chills. Now I know why. It is the devil, conning and baffling. He plays on our weakness' and comes in an addiction form. He takes our health, our kids, our families, hurts the ones we love, takes away the ability to love, the ability to progress, doesn't allow us to feel and move forward. It strips us of our dignity, self-respect and leaves us feeling angry and alone. Addictions of any type are the devil in disguise, to fool us and make us believe things that are not true. Scripture says: "the devil is the father of lies".

Sobriety to me, is Jesus in disguise. Whatever we lost we can get back, restore and renew relationships, gain back trust, get a job or an even better one, lets us feel our feelings and actually want to work through them. We get back everything the devil once took plus a whole lot more. We get our life back and a better one. It gives us an appreciation we never had before and what others can not even comprehend because they have not been through what we have been through. We gain a love and compassion we never thought we were capable of having. It gives us contentment and peace. It can turn a monster back into a loving and caring person.

Just because I am changing my life and my inner-self I am still far from perfect. I do not go to church every Sunday. Most Sundays but not every Sunday. I do not read my bible everyday. I swear. I have temper-tantrums. I am human. I do not try and pretend I am all holy because I am not. Unless God plans on making me a nun, I will never be all-holy. I am a sinner. I sin everyday. A sin is a sin. One sin is not more horrible than the next in God's eyes. However, I am not even close to what I used to be. Slowly God is turning my mess into a a message.

I was my own worse enemy and it showed. I love myself now. I actually can say if I did not know me I would want to be around me.

I would want to be my friend. I would want me for a mother. I would want me for a wife. I would want me for a daughter. I have goals. I will reach them and I will make it. With the love and support of my family and God on my side, I was-CARRIED!

Epilogue

Writing this book was extremely painful. Reliving my past has caused nightmares, flashbacks, stress and frustration. Upon completion of this book-I relapsed.

My relapse signs were very clear. I had stopped going to AA, I skipped the previous weeks church service, was negative and had mood swings. I had become so full of myself I thought I could do it on my own. I ignored my relapse signs and did nothing to prevent them.

It was God who had helped me to progress and as soon as I reached my goal- I spoke to God less, I relied on him less-I prayed less-the gospel music in my car turned to R &

B. As a result of forgetting who brought me up-I came tumbling back down.

Thankfully my relapse with alcohol only lasted five hours, but in that five hours relapse-I broke my families heart, again. I re-inflicted pain in the wounds that were beginning to heal. That is what hurts the most.

I do not regret writing this book. Hopefully thru my deepest secrets, my dark and shady past another person will find the courage to get help, make a better choice and know they are not alone. Knowing true happiness and a fullfilling life are out there makes this all very much worth it.

Romans 8:18

> What we suffer now is nothing compared to the glory He will reveal to us later.